MADE POSSIBLE WITH
FUNDING FROM THE

SUFFOLK COUNTY PBA

868 Church Street
Bohemia, New York 11716

MY DAD'S A HERO...

MY

DAD'S

A

COP

Published by Probity Press ISBN 0-9667454-0-X First Edition 2012
1. Children. 2. Police — Title 2012

This book is available at quantity discounts for bulk purchases.
For information call 631-724-5522

PROBITY PRESS
New York

Our dad is *different.*
He knows a lot of bad people.

He sees a lot of bad things.

Mommy worries about
what daddy does.

My Dad's a **COP**!

Dad **HELPS** people who are lost.

Dad *helps* people **feel safe**.

Dad helps people when they are **hurt**.

Dad helps people who are *in trouble*.

Dad helps people learn to **follow the rules.**

And sometimes Dad just **waits** and WAITS and waits...

But Dad is EXTRA CAREFUL.

Dad works at night sometimes, and during the DAY sometimes. He gets real tired some days.

One time, Mom and Dad were talking *softly*.

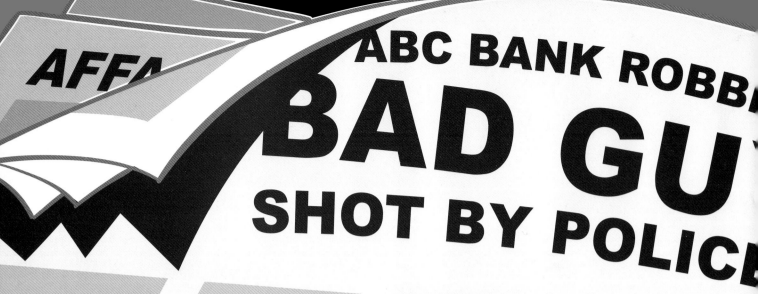

AFFA

ABC BANK ROBB[ERY]

BAD GU[Y]
SHOT BY POLICE

OLICE CASE

ABC ROBBERY SCEN[E]

Dad's name was IN THE NEWSPAPER.
I think he shot a **bad guy**.

It took a LONG TIME, but soon everything was over. And Dad was back to being our SAME OLD DADDY again.

My Dad's a Hero…My Dad's a Cop
A Parent's Guide to Teaching from this Book

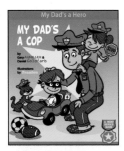

Your child is sure to be excited about a book devoted to his or her parent's job. We suggest you start by sitting down and reading the book to your child as you would any children's book. Each page can be a starting point for discussion about your job, or elicit questions from your child about what you do. Your son/daughter may ask you outright, "Do you do that?" Take your time and answer your child's questions honestly. It is also possible that your son or daughter may simply sit quietly, enjoying the story, the illustrations, and the time they're spending with you. Bring the book out often to read again – once a month for younger kids, and three or four times a year for older kids

Police work is a job that is different from many adults' jobs, and this page sets the stage for this idea. Use the text to encourage a lot of questions:

- How is being a police officer different than other jobs?
  - o Uniform, badge, gun.
  - o Military-like structure (paramilitary) – "kind of like being in the army."
  - o Shift work – working when other fathers are home, like weekends and holidays.
- What types of bad people could Dad know?
  - o Robbers and crooks
  - o People who break laws
- What types of bad things does Daddy see? This requires some care. You know your child. You do not want to overwhelm him. You do want to educate him.
  - o Car accidents
  - o People being mean to each other (a domestic incident)
  - o People who are scared – like lost children
- Why does Mommy worry about Daddy? This is an opportunity to normalize the worry that you children may see and experience. It's a chance to let them know they have permission to tell you or their mother how they feel. Often children will keep certain feelings to themselves, especially if they believe that talking about them will distress you.
  - o People worry about each other because they love and care about each other.
  - o Police work can be dangerous, so that is why we are well-trained and have lots of tools. Do you know some of the tools police have?
  - o Mommy and Daddy worry about you too when you are not feeling well, or when you are sad. It is okay to worry, but then you need to think about other things.

Helping people is a major part of police work. Children relate to this. A good discussion can start with the many ways both adults and children could get lost:

- Where do you think children or grownups can get lost?
  - o A store, mall, park, neighborhood, etc.
- What should a person do if they get lost?
  - o Try to find a policeman, other uniformed person, a mother with children, or go into a store.

- Why do people feel safe when a policeman is near?
  - They know he/she will protect them.
  - "Bad guys" stay away from places they see police.
  - They can ask a policeman for help. Someone who's lost can ask for directions, or if they are feeling sick, a policeman will help them to get to a doctor.

This section can help a child see that police work can be very different than what they see on TV. TV emphasizes the high danger element of police work. But the more important part of police work is the aid and comfort police offer people.

- What are different ways people can be hurt?
  - Car accidents, injuries in the home, animal bites, injury on playgrounds or in parks, or even a woman having a baby!
- What does a police officer do when they go to help an injured person?
  - Police officers know first aid and have special training.
  - Many are emergency medical technicians.
  - They call an ambulance or even drive people to the hospital.
  - They control crowds of people so everyone gets the attention they need.
- How does Dad help people feel better?
  - Sometimes people need comfort.
  - Policemen care about the people in the community they patrol.
  - Just knowing that someone is now here who can help calms people down.
  - People sometimes don't know what to do and get scared, but a policeman often has good answers that help people.
  - Give examples from you own work of helping people.

This section can lead to discussion about the types of trouble people can find themselves in.

- What types of trouble do you think people can find themselves in?
  - Being lost
  - Car broken down
  - Being homeless
  - Needing a doctor
- Why are rules important?
  - They keep us safe.
  - They keep things running smoothly, like having to raise your hand when the teacher asks a question.
  - They help us keep friends (we aren't rude, we take turns).
  - They help us be good people (we don't steal, we are polite).

This section starts a discussion about how police work can be dangerous. It also brings up the specter of people doing bad things.

- Why do you think people do bad things?
  - They want things they don't have.
  - They don't want to work hard to earn things.
  - They never learned right from wrong.
- How are the police in the picture keeping as safe as they can?
  - One officer is staying behind the car (taking cover).
  - The other officer is keeping a safe distance while he sees what needs to be done.

  (Police are trained to develop a plan and not just rush into things!)

  - They work in teams.
  - They have the right tools.
  - They are trained and they are smart.
- Why do we need to catch bad people?
- What would happen if there were no police to catch the bad people?
- Do you see all the tools for police to keep safe in the picture? (You can talk about how cops keep safe.)
  - Multiple people; teamwork and planning
  - Radio in car to keep in touch and get help
  - Bullet proof vests
  - Discuss other police assets:
    - Police dogs, helicopters, Tasers, and handcuffs

This picture lightens the discussion and transitions into discussion about all the different things police do, even if Dad doesn't do any of them. You can start by asking if they know that police officers have many different jobs. Then, you can guide the discussion to talk about the different "teams" of police officers that we call "units" (or Bureaus), like:

Canine; aviation; marine bureau; Emergency Services (SWAT); crime scene, detectives, undercover officers – the list can be as long as your child is interested.

This picture can start a conversation as simple as defining and describing what a stakeout is (a very popular scene in TV shows and movies). It can lead to good discussion about how police work is often very different than what you see on TV or even in the papers. This picture gives parents a chance to discuss the more mundane and even boring aspects of police work. It allows children to see that their dad does not spend his whole shift faced with tension and danger. This realistic portrayal of some aspects of police work helps to normalize the job in the child's mind. This will help with some of the secondary stress issues that children of police officers can experience.

The general public often doesn't understand the need for police officers to make quick decisions, so this is also something to explain to your child. We call this "Burst Stress," or the need to go from 0 to 100 miles an hour in a split second. In almost all other jobs, you have a lot of time to make a decision. If you make a mistake, you can correct it. Often neither is true in police work! Discussion questions can include:

- Why do you think police officers have to make quick decisions?
- What types of things do we have to decide fast?
- Why is it important that we work hard not to make a mistake?
- What tools to police have to he careful?

Shift work is a major difference between police work and many other jobs. These pictures introduce this topic, which is very important for family life. Most children have friends whose fathers work Monday through Friday, 9 to 5. Police work odd hours, weekends, and holidays. Disruption of sleep patterns can affect the officer. Disruption of cultural routines can affect the family. Questions for this segment include:

- Why do police officers have to work at night when most other parents are home?
- Why do police have to work on weekends and holidays?
- How have our holidays been different because Daddy is a police officer?
    - o Celebrate different days/times
    - o Daddy is not at some family events
    - o Sometimes Daddy is not at the child's events
- What is the best thing about Daddy/Mommy working weekends and nights?
- What is the worst thing?

The next series of pictures introduces the concept that at times police work can be so stressful that it has an effect on Mom or Dad that the child can see. Some very important discussion can be established here.

- Have you ever thought Dad was upset because of his work?
- Why did you think Dad was upset?
- How do you feel when you see that Dad is upset?
- What do you think of asking Dad why he is upset?
    - o Would that be a good idea?
    - o How would you ask?

This picture deals with Critical Incidents faced by police officers. It is gentle in that it does not bring up death, but it does talk about a shooting, which is something that would be likely to end up in the newspaper. Simply seeing his or her father in the newspaper can be a stressful event for a child. Consider your child's age and maturity level when presenting the discussion questions below.

- Have you ever thought about Dad having to shoot someone?
- Why would a police officer have to shoot someone?
- Have you ever thought of other scary things that might happen to Dad/Mom?
    - ** At this point, review how much equipment and training police have to keep themselves safe!
- How do you think Dad/Mom will feel after something so scary happens?
- How would you feel if you saw it in the newspaper?
- How do you think your friends would react?

- What would they say to you?
- What would your teachers say to you?
- What would be on the internet?

A Critical Incident might have some effect on the state of the family. People change in the face of trauma. If children are aware of this fact, it can prevent them from blaming themselves for their parent's distress. Questions include:

- Do you think Dad/Mom might act differently after something scary happened to him/her?
    - Why do you think people act differently after something scary happens?
    - How do you think people should act?
- After something scary happens, what should people do?
    - Talk to their family.
    - Take some time off.
    - Be with their family to remember how much family loves each other!
    - Talk with someone who really knows how to help with scary things!

We end the book reminding kids that regardless of what happens, their parents love them and things are will work out. Bad things get better. They are encouraged to see their parents, their home, and their family as strong, and as something that will always be there for them. Some questions include:

We end the book reminding kids that regardless of what happens, their parents love them and things are will work out. Bad things get better. They are encouraged to see their parents, their home, and their family as strong, and as something that will always be there for them. Some questions include:

And finally, the children come to the conclusion…